Fancy NANCY Sees Stars

by Jane O'Connor

cover illustration by Robin Preiss Glasser

interior illustrations by Ted Enik

HarperCollins *Children's Books*

Stars are so fascinating.

(That's a fancy word

for interesting.)

I love how they sparkle in the sky.

Tonight is our class trip.

Yes! It's a class trip at night!

We are going to the planetarium.

That is a museum

about stars and planets.

Ms Glass tells us,

"The show starts at eight.

We will all meet there."

I smile at my friend Robert.

My parents are taking Robert and me.

Then Ms Glass asks,

"What star is closest to Earth?"

That's easy.

It's the sun.

"What do you call stars
that make a picture?"
asks Ms Glass.
Robert and Bree have both forgotten.
"I know, I know," I say.
"A constellation."

Ms Glass nods.

On the wall are pictures.

There's the hunter and the crab

and the Big Dipper.

It looks like a big spoon.

CANCER
THE
CRAB

ORION
THE
HUNTER

We will see all of them at the show.

I can hardly wait.

At home, Robert and I
put glow-in-the-dark stickers
on our T-shirts.
Mine has the Big Dipper.
Robert has the hunter on his.

We spin my mobile

and watch the planets orbit the sun.

(Orbit is a fancy word.

It means to travel in a circle.)

Then we pretend to orbit

until we get dizzy.

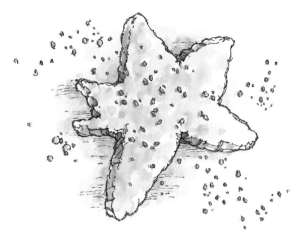

Later, we bake star cookies.

Sprinkles make them sparkle.

"The sun is a star,"

I tell my sister.

"It is the closest star,

so we see it in the day."

After dinner,

we wait for the baby-sitter.

She is very late.

Dad says not to worry.

We have plenty of time.

At last we get in the car.

Drip, drip, drip.

It is raining.

The rain comes down
harder and harder.
Dad drives slower and slower.
It is getting later and later.

A policeman comes over.

"The road is closed,"

he tells my parents.

"There is too much water."

Oh no!

There are cars in front of us.

There are cars behind us.

We are stuck!

"The show is starting soon!"

Robert says.

"We will not make it."

Drip, drip, drip goes the rain.

Drip, drip, drip go my tears.

Robert and I are so sad.

We do not even want any cookies.

At last the cars move

and the rain stops.

But it is too late.

The night sky show is over.

By the time we get home,

the sky is full of stars.

They are brilliant!

(That's a fancy word

for shiny and bright.)

I get a brilliant idea.

(Brilliant also means very smart.)

We can have

our own night sky show.

My parents get my sister.

We set up beach chairs.

Mum lights candles.

Dad puts the cookies on a tray.

We eat alfresco.

(That's fancy for eating outdoors.)

We watch the stars.

We see the North Star.

We see the Big Dipper.

All at once,

something zooms across the sky.

"A shooting star," Dad says.

"Make a wish!"

I tell Dad it is not a star.

It is a meteor.

But I make a wish anyway.